STEWART (PAUL)
The Watch-frog

For Anna

THE WATCH-FROG
A CORGI PUPS BOOK: 0 552 54826 X

First publication in Great Britain by Corgi Pups Books,
an imprint of Random House Children's Books

This edition published 2003

1 3 5 7 9 10 8 6 4 2

Set in 18/25 pt Bembo MT Schoolbook by
Falcon Oast Graphic Art Ltd.

Corgi Pups Books are published by Random House Children's Books,
61–63 Uxbridge Road, London W5 5SA,
a division of The Random House Group Ltd,
in Australia by Random House Australia (Pty) Ltd,
20 Alfred Street, Milsons Point, Sydney, NSW 2061, Australia,
in New Zealand by Random House New Zealand Ltd,
18 Poland Road, Glenfield, Auckland 10, New Zealand
and in South Africa by Random House (Pty) Ltd,
Endulini, 5A Jubilee Road, Parktown 2193, South Africa

THE RANDOM HOUSE GROUP Limited Reg. No. 954009

A CIP catalogue record for this book
is available from the British Library.

Printed and bound in Great Britain by
Cox & Wyman Ltd, Reading, Berkshire.

Contents

Series Reading Consultant: Prue Goodwin,
Reading and Language Information Centre,
University of Reading

Chapter One

"Go away!" Looby shouted
down from her bedroom window.
"Go on. Hop it!"

The frog took no notice.
"*Ribbit!*" it went. "*Ribbit!*"

Looby slammed the window shut, climbed back into bed and wrapped her pillow round her head. But she could still hear the frog croaking loudly in the garden pond.

"*Ribbit! Ribbit! Ribbit!*"

Louise Mitchell – or Looby, as everyone knew her – was eight years old. She lived with her mum and dad in a tall, thin terraced house. Looby had the back bedroom, where it was supposed to be quiet.

It had been – until the frog arrived.

Now, each morning at four o'clock on the dot, the frog would start croaking. It was still croaking when she went to bed in the evening. The awful noise had been going on for five days.

Looby was fed up – and very, very tired.

Every Friday afternoon Looby's grandfather would pick her up from school. Usually he would greet her with, "Looby! My favourite granddaughter!" – which was a sort of joke, since she was his *only* granddaughter.

On this particular Friday, however – a week after the arrival of the infuriating frog – Grandad's first words were quite different.

"Looby!" he said. "There are deep, dark circles under your eyes. What have you been doing? You look *so* tired."

"I am," Looby admitted, and yawned. "Exhausted!"

"Let's get home," said Grandad, "and you can tell me all about it. I've got us a special treat this afternoon," he added. "Jam doughnuts!"

"Oh, Looby!" Grandad laughed, when Looby had finished telling him all about the frog. "Is that all?"

"But you don't understand," said Looby. "It's deafening."

"Frogs *can* be loud in May and June," Grandad nodded. "Especially the males. He's calling for a mate." He frowned thoughtfully and rubbed his chin. "Un-less . . ." he said slowly.

Looby looked at him. "Unless what?"

Grandad sat down and drew his chair closer. "Unless it's not a frog at all," he said.

"Not a frog?" said Looby. "Of course it's a frog. I've seen it."

"Oh, I'm sure it *looks* like a frog," said Grandad. "But why should it be croaking during the day? That's very unusual."

He drew closer. His voice turned to a hushed whisper. "What if it's a person who's been turned into a frog by a wicked witch? You remember the story of the Frog Prince . . ."

"Oh, Grandad," said Looby, disappointed. "I'm too old for fairy tales about wicked witches and magic spells."

Grandad leaned back.
"Perhaps you are," he said. "But
just because you no longer
believe in magic, it doesn't mean
it no longer exists." And he
pulled a shiny coin from her ear.

Looby laughed. Then, remembering what the princess in the fairy tale had done, she said, "And I'll tell you this, Grandad. Magic or no magic, I do *not* intend to kiss it. Ever!"

Grandad smiled mysteriously. "We'll see," he said.

Chapter Two

Dear old Grandad, thought
Looby as she walked home.

To him, she was still the same
wide-eyed little girl who had
been enchanted by his magical
tales. But Looby was big now.

She knew the frog in her garden
was just that – a frog. And a
horribly loud one at that.

On Saturday morning when
the frog woke her – at four
o'clock on the dot! – Looby
decided to take action.

Ribbit
Ribbit
Ribbit

She went downstairs, out of the
back door and into the garden.
The frog was on a lily-pad in
the middle of the pond, croaking
for all it was worth.

"*Ribbit! Rib—*"

"I'll teach you to wake me up so early!" Looby cried as she seized it in her hand. She stomped across the lawn to the back fence and tossed it into the stream which ran behind the row of gardens.

"*Ribbit!*" said the frog.

"Just go away!" Looby
shouted and marched back to
the house – and her warm, cosy,
and finally *quiet* bed.

It didn't stay quiet for
long. By six o'clock
the frog was back
and croaking louder
than ever.

"That's it!" Looby said. She
got dressed and went
down to the
kitchen.

"You're up early," said Mum. "Did that frog wake you up again?"

"Yes, it did!" said Looby crossly. "Twice! And I'm going to make sure it never does again."

"Oh, Looby," said Mum, "I hope you're not going to hurt it."

"Of course I'm not," she said. "But I'm going to catch it and then we're going to take it a long, long way away . . ."

Looby had decided to release the frog at Lidden Lake, a beauty spot about half a mile away. With the frog inside a plastic sandwich-box, she and her mum climbed into the car and set off. Five minutes later they were standing at the water's edge.

"Would you like some bread
for the ducks?" Mum asked.

"First things first," said Looby.
She opened the lid of the
sandwich-box and tipped it up.

The frog plopped down into the water. "Bye–bye, froggy," said Looby as the frog kicked its legs and disappeared. "And good riddance!"

That evening Looby lay in bed listening to the quiet. "At last!" she muttered happily. And she rolled over and fell into a deep, deep sleep.

Chapter Three

"*Ribbit! Ribbit!*"

Looby's eyes snapped open.
She looked at the clock. It was
four o'clock – and the frog was
back!

But how had it returned from so far away? And so quickly? And how had it found its way? And, most important of all, *why*?

"*Ribbit! Ribbit!*"

Was it a super-frog? Looby wondered. Or might Grandad have been right all along?

"*Ribbit! Ribbit!*"

"Don't be ridiculous!" Looby told herself. "Spawn, tadpole, frog – that's the way it happens. But human being to frog . . ." She shook her head. "It's impossible."

"*Ribbit! Rib—*"

The frog abruptly stopped croaking. The silence that followed seemed to echo round the room.

Looby ran to the window.
And there, next to the pond, was
Pugsy – next door's big ginger
tom – with two froggy legs
sticking out of his mouth.

For a moment Looby considered doing nothing about it. But only for a moment. No frog – however noisy – deserved to be eaten by Pugsy.

She tore downstairs and into the garden. "Pugsy!" she shouted. "Put it down!"

The cat purred. The frog kicked its legs weakly.

"PUGSY!"

Looby grabbed him by the scruff of his neck and eased his jaws open. The frog tumbled to the ground, where it lay still. There was blood on one of its front legs.

"Pugsy, you naughty cat!" said Looby, and shooed him away.

Then she picked up the limp, trembling creature. "Oh, froggy," she said, "I never wanted *this* to happen. You poor little thing."

And before Looby knew quite
what she was doing, she had put
the frog to her puckered lips and
planted a tiny kiss right on the
end of its mouth.

"Thank you," the frog
croaked weakly.

Looby started back in surprise.
"I . . . I . . . I . . ." she stammered.

"But please put me down," the frog continued. "Your hands are unpleasantly warm."

Looby did as she was told. The kiss hadn't turned the frog into a handsome prince – but it had made it speak.

"H–have you had a magic spell put on you?" she asked.

The frog nodded.

"By a wicked witch?" said Looby.

"The wickedest!" said the frog.

"But . . . this is just what my grandad told me," said Looby.

"Then your
grandad is a
wise man,"
said the frog.
"Not many
people believe
in such things
nowadays. *I* didn't . . ." it added,
with a long, sorrowful sigh.

 "But what happened?"
said Looby.

"It's a long story," said
the frog.

"Let me get this straight," said
Looby, when the frog had

finished. "You're not a frog at all, you're a twelve-year-old boy who was at a seaside adventure camp."

"You've got it," said the frog. "My parents send me there every year while they're off trekking up the Amazon."

"And last Sunday, while you were diving off the coast, you bumped into a witch."

"A *water*-witch," the frog corrected her.

"And *she* turned you into a frog."

"Yes," said the frog, and shuddered. "I can still see her long sharp nails and horrible bloodshot eyes. And that voice!

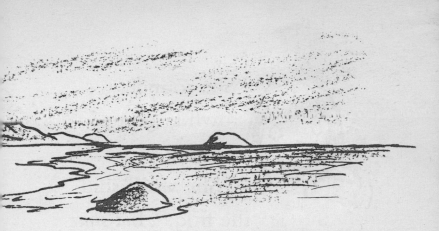

I'll teach you to come poking your
nose into every whelk and barnacle,
and scaring the fish, she screeched."

"She sounds awful," gasped Looby.

"She was!" said the frog. "*And since you're so keen on watching others, Mr Froggy-man, she went on, that's exactly what you shall be. A watch-frog! And so you shall remain until the time when you help someone out!* Then she cackled with laughter, snapped her

fingers and – *kazam!* – I was
here, as you see me now. I
think I'm meant to be *your*
watch-frog."

"Just my luck," said Looby. "I haven't slept properly for a week."

"Yes, I'm sorry about that," said the frog. "I was just trying to get your attention."

Looby nodded. "I suppose I'd have done exactly the same thing," she said, then added, "But won't anyone be missing you?"

 The frog shook its head. "It's all been a bit of a mix-up," it explained. "My parents think I'm at the camp. The camp thinks my parents came to pick me up. Somehow, I've got to turn back into my real self before they  get back and find me gone."

"And when's that?" Looby asked.

"In eight days," said the frog.

"So, before they do," said
Looby, remembering the
water-witch's words, "you've
got to help me out."

"Exactly," said the frog.
"And that's not easy when

you're small, squidgy and only
eight centimetres long. I haven't
a clue what to do."

"Me neither," Looby admitted.
"But one thing's certain," she
said as she noticed Pugsy sitting
on the fence, licking his lips.

"You can't stay out here. There's
an old aquarium in the lean-to.
I'll get some gravel and pond-
weed, and put you in that."

"Thank you," said the frog
for a second time.

By the time Looby had found
the aquarium and washed it
out, she was beginning to yawn.
It was, after all, still only five
o'clock in the morning.

"Leave the gravel and pond-weed for now," said the frog. "Get some more sleep. You look shattered!"

"And whose fault is that?" said Looby crossly.

"I told you I was sorry," said the frog. "I'll be quiet from now on, I promise."

Chapter Four

Looby slept till ten o'clock that Sunday morning, when her mum woke her up with a cup of tea. "It's a lovely day," she said, "You don't want to waste it all." She smiled. "Though I'm glad you got a good night's sleep for once."

"So am I, Mum," said Looby.
"Oh, but I had the weirdest
dream. All about a talking
frog . . ."

"That reminds me," said her
mum. "What are you planning
to do with that frog in the
aquarium?"

"Frog?"
Looby
spluttered.
"Aquarium?
It can't be . . ."

She leaped out of bed and
raced downstairs. And sure
enough, there in the lean-to

where she hoped she'd only *dreamed* she'd left it, was the frog.

Looby's head spun. Was she going crazy? Since the frog was in the aquarium, it couldn't have been a dream. But if it *wasn't* a dream . . .

She picked up the frog. "Can you speak?" she said.

The frog remained silent.

"Well, *can* you?" she said. "I didn't even ask your name."

Still nothing. Not a word – not even a croaky little *ribbit*.

Looby didn't know what to think, but with Pugsy still on the prowl, she couldn't return the frog to the pond. So she equipped its new home with the

gravel and pond-weed, and
brought it slugs, bugs and worms
to eat. Then she carried the
whole lot up to her bedroom
and placed it on her desk.

"But you'd better remember
your promise!" she said.

The frog did remember. The days
passed, and not once did it wake
her up or stop her going to sleep.

"The mating season's over," Grandad explained that Friday. "That's why it's so quiet."

But Looby was not so sure. She couldn't forget her dream – if it *was* a dream.

Whatever the reason, the frog was quiet now – and so it might have stayed if it hadn't been for Dad's little accident.

"*RIBBIT! RIBBIT!*"
Looby sat bolt upright in bed.

It was pitch-black
outside. She looked at
her clock. "Twenty to
one!" she groaned.

"*RIBBIT! RIBBIT!*"

"What's the matter?" said
Looby.

The frog jumped up and down
in the aquarium. "*RIBBIT!*" it
cried. "**RIBBIT!!**"

And then Looby smelt it . . .
Gas!

"MUM! DAD!" she bellowed.
"I CAN SMELL GAS!"

Two fire engines, an ambulance
and a man from the gas board
arrived minutes after Mum's 999
call.

It didn't take them long to
find the leak. Looby's dad was
called back into the house.

"Someone been doing a spot of DIY, have they?" said the chief fire-fighter.

"This is highly irregular," said the man from the gas board. "Boilers must only be installed by qualified fitters."

"I know . . . I thought . . . That is, I didn't . . ." Dad muttered.

"Everything's safe now, sir," said the chief fire-fighter. "Just remember, some jobs are best left to professionals."

When the fire-fighters, ambulance crew and the man from the gas board had finally all gone, Looby's mum turned to her. "Oh, Looby," she said. "Thank heavens you woke up when you did."

"It was the frog," said Looby.

"The *watch-frog* . . ."

Suddenly, the frog's words came back to her. She charged back up to her bedroom. The aquarium was empty. The frog was nowhere to be seen. Then she noticed them . . .

Footprints.

Big, wet footprints.

Big, wet, *flipper*-shaped footprints crossing the carpet from the desk to the door.

Looby followed them along the landing, down the stairs and through the kitchen to the back door. Outside, the footprints continued down the garden path and away.

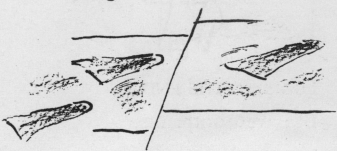

The watch-frog *had* managed to help someone out, she realized. He'd saved their lives. And the wicked witch's curse had been removed.

"Goodbye, watch-frog – whoever you are," Looby whispered. "And thank *you*!"

THE END